Are You Sad, Little Bear?

For Sarah, who shines in our hearts,
with love   R.R.

To my Granddad
Iain Alisdair Robertson Macnaughton   T.N.

Text copyright © 2009 Rachel Rivett
Illustrations copyright © 2009 Tina Macnaughton
This edition copyright © 2009 Lion Hudson

Published by Lion Children's Books
an imprint of
Lion Hudson plc
Wilkinson House, Jordan Hill Road,
Oxford OX2 8DR, England
www.lionhudson.com/lionchildrens

Hardback ISBN 978 0 7459 6137 8
Paperback ISBN 978 0 7459 6430 0
e-ISBN 978 0 7459 6779 0

First edition 2009
This edition 2013

A catalogue record of this book is available from
the British Library

Printed and bound in China, March 2013, LH06

Are You Sad, Little Bear?

A book about learning to say goodbye

Rachel Rivett
Illustrated by Tina Macnaughton

LION
CHILDREN'S

Little Bear huddled close to his mother in the chill morning light.

His mother's voice was gentle. 'Are you sad, Little Bear?'

'Yes,' he said. 'I am.'

Only the day before, Grandmother Bear had waved farewell. Then she had walked away for ever, as old bears do.

'I'm sad, too,' said Mother Bear.

Little Bear looked up at her. 'Why can't things always stay the same?'

His mother nuzzled him gently. 'Perhaps there are answers in the Wildwood.'

'Yes.' Little Bear stood up. 'I'll see if I can find them.'

In the sky, the swallows soared and swooped. 'Farewell,
Little Bear. Winter's coming. We're flying to warmer
lands.'

'O Swallow,' called Little Bear, 'are you sad to leave
your nests?'

'No, no,' she called. 'Our other home is calling us.
Can you hear?'

In the woods, the wind chased the leaves from the trees.

'O Tree,' Little Bear called. 'Are you sad to lose your leaves?'

The tree smiled and swayed. 'Why should I be sad, Little Bear? I love this time of letting go. Think about it. Have you ever seen me look more beautiful?'

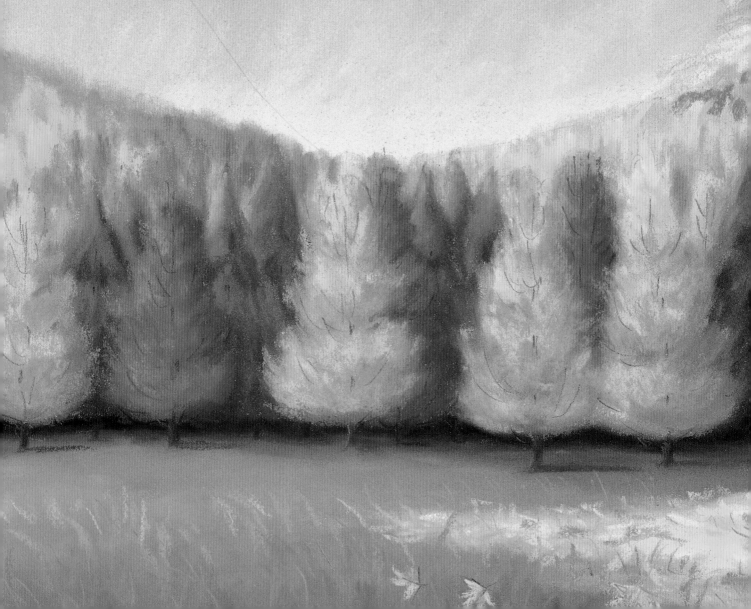

A flying leaf caught Little Bear
on the nose. 'O Leaf,' he smiled,
'you've left your tree. I thought
you'd be sad about that!'

The leaves whirled wildly around him. 'Do we look sad?'
they giggled. 'Come and play!'

Little Bear ran to the stream for a drink.

'O Stream,' he asked, 'are you sad when your water leaves to join the clouds?'

The stream sparkled and sang. 'Oh no, I'm glad! Look! A part of me can fly.'

As Little Bear wandered on, he saw Dormouse
already curling up in her winter nest.
  'Goodnight, Little Bear,' she said dreamily.
'I'm soooo tired. See you in the spring.'

As the sun sank lower in the sky, Little Bear hurried home.
All the daytime creatures were hurrying too. 'Goodnight,
Little Bear,' they called. 'Sweet dreams.'
  'Goodnight.'

And then a new question occurred to Little Bear. 'O Sun, do you die at the end of every day? Are you sad to leave us?' The sun glowed. 'Is that how it seems, little one? No, I don't die. When I set in your sky, I rise in another. Just because you can't see me, it doesn't mean I'm not there. Remember that.'

Then Little Bear glimpsed the silver of the newborn moon.
 'O Moon, you're always changing, and sometimes you completely disappear. Are you sad to leave?'
 The voice of the moon was soft. 'I don't really disappear, little one. But sometimes my dance brings me so close to the sun that I can't be seen for his brightness. No, Little Bear, I'm not sad about that. I love to return to the sun.'

'Little Bear.' His mother called him softly. 'I found sweet honey in the Wildwood. What did you find, little one?'

'Lots of things!' Little Bear ran to hug her fiercely. 'Nothing is as I thought.'

Mother Bear kissed him gently. 'And are you still sad, little one?'

Little Bear thought. 'Not so sad. Now my sadness is full of wonder.'

As night came, even though Little Bear couldn't see them, all his friends shone in his heart like bright stars in the dark. And as he looked up at the host of sparkling stars in the heavens, he felt that he and his mother and his grandmother were also shining in the Great Heart that holds everything for always.

Other titles from Lion Children's Books

Little Grey and the Great Mystery *Rachel Rivett*

I Imagine *Rachel Rivett*